LEGENDS OF CHIMA™

BEWARE OF THE WOLVES

Scholastic Inc.

"The Hollow Tree," "Lone Wolf," and "Worriz's Challenge"
written by Greg Farshtey

Illustrated by Ameet Studio

ISBN 978-0-545-60669-1

12 11 10 9 8 7 6 5 4 3 2 1   13 14 15 16 17 18/0

Printed in the U.S.A.   40
This edition first Scholastic printing, September 2013

TABLE OF CONTENTS

I am LaGravis, king of the Lion Tribe. We Lions guard Chima's greatest treasure—the CHI. Let me tell you about my world.

Thousands of years ago, Chima was an unspoiled land filled with lush jungles and simple animals that lived in peace and harmony.

Then, one day, a mighty lightning bolt struck Chima. The ground shook, and a giant rock called Mount Cavora rose from the ground. Magical waterfalls spilled from this floating mountain, filling a river on the land below with a mysterious life-force called CHI. Some animals drank the energized water and transformed into two-legged, more complex creatures. The CHI enabled our ancestors to develop advanced technology and build amazing structures. Today, CHI powers everything we have created. It can also enhance our strength, abilities, and instincts, if used wisely.

As the first to drink CHI, we Lions guard the precious orbs and share them fairly with every tribe in Chima. However, not long ago, the sneaky Crocodiles decided that they wanted all of the CHI for themselves. Joined by the Wolves and Ravens, they challenged us to take control of the CHI. And a fierce battle began!

Luckily, we have true friends standing by our side, as well. . . .

The Eagles are one of the wisest, most innovative tribes in Chima. They are also our closest allies. Living high above the clouds on Chima's mysterious rock spires, the Eagles have a unique outlook on the world. They are observers and thinkers, clever but also a little bit lofty. If you let them start talking, you may have to listen to their philosophical theories for hours on end. But they are great fighters and have mastered fierce aerial assaults to counter any enemy.

When Cragger, the Crocodile King, led his army to attack the Lion Temple, I had no choice but to call upon our friends for help. The Eagles were the first to arrive to the battlefield. They knew that we Lions have been guarding the CHI for centuries to keep the natural balance of Chima, and that we have always shared it equally with everyone— even with those tribes that aren't our allies. The Eagles understood that balance must be preserved for the sake of all of Chima.

Supported by our winged friends, we hope to maintain the ancient order and protect our world from untold calamities should all of the CHI
fall in Cragger's greedy claws.

ERIS

Eris is an intelligent young Eagle and the daughter of one of her tribe's Ruling Council Members. She is also the best friend of my son, Laval. Unlike some of her more eccentric tribe members, she is extremely focused and quick-witted. She loves adventures and puzzles, and she can tell stories like no other creature. Eris is a brilliant tactician. What she lacks in strength, she makes up for with smarts.

Eris believes strongly in peace and doesn't always understand creatures who want to fight instead of talk. She's the first to lend a hand and the last to leave a friend in need. You can always count on Eris. Just don't let her corner you and tell you jokes—a lot of them aren't as funny as she thinks.

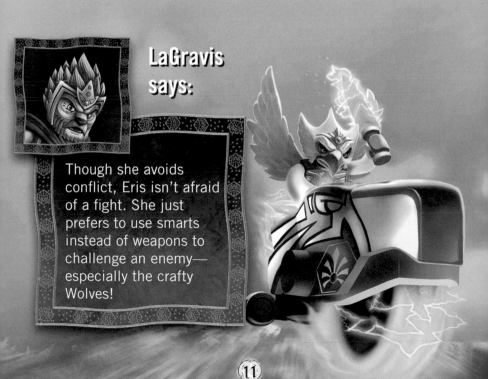

LaGravis says:

Though she avoids conflict, Eris isn't afraid of a fight. She just prefers to use smarts instead of weapons to challenge an enemy—especially the crafty Wolves!

THE WOLVES

The Wolves live in the forest and are one of Chima's craftiest tribes. They are also the Crocodiles' allies in the battle for the CHI, though even the Crocs know that the Wolves can't be trusted farther than their snouts.

Unlike other tribes in Chima, the Wolves are a traveling group and never stay long in one place. Their convoys are made up of rugged battle vehicles, and they sleep in tightly packed piles so they can cram as many warriors into their "homes on wheels" as possible.

Everyone in the pack is somebody's brother, sister, or cousin, and they will do anything for one another. Group decisions are usually arrived at easily and unanimously, so there is no real need for leaders. However, the Wolves' traveling caravans often bring them into contact, and conflict, with other creatures. So someone in the tribe has to handle negotiations. Worriz the Wolf was given this role because he was considered "the most personable."

The Wolves are ferocious fighters, but they have no honor. They calculate the risk involved in their actions and are not afraid to leave an ally behind if it means they will remain safe. For them it's not about pride or glory. It's about getting the job done with a minimum amount of sacrifice.

WORRIZ

Worriz is the Wolf Tribe's lead negotiator, and he is the closest thing that the wild Wolves have to a "responsible ruler." In reality, Worriz is a vicious and ruthless creature who loves a well-executed betrayal. But he is able to disguise his true nature long enough to fool others. He can even occasionally fake a bit of "charm" when needed.

When he was much younger, Worriz was friends with many different animals, including my son, Laval. But his personality changed as he grew. He became aggressive and double-dealing. Now Worriz claims he was only friends with the other species because "he didn't know any better."

Worriz believes an alliance with the Crocodiles against the Lions can be profitable for his tribe, so his current "best friend" is Cragger, the Crocodile King. Worriz seeks personal revenge against Laval for a Speedor joust that ended badly. He also wants to rule all of Chima, should Cragger ever fall—or be pushed—from power.

TURN THE PAGE FOR **THREE** EXCITING LEGENDS OF CHIMA™ STORIES!

THE HOLLOW TREE

Eris flew over the treetops. It was a quiet, peaceful day in Chima . . . or so it seemed. But Eris knew better. She was on a mission straight from the Ruling Council. A hidden danger was lurking somewhere in the forest, and it was her job to seek it out.

I can't believe things have gotten so bad, so quickly, Eris thought to herself as she flew. Just a few weeks ago, the Crocodiles had attacked the Lions for the first time for control of the CHI. Now they had enlisted the help of the Wolves to continue their fight—and the Ravens, too! The battle for CHI was growing larger by the day.

The Crocs have to be crazy to trust the Wolves, Eris thought. *But there's no doubt the pack is very dangerous.*

The Wolves were one of the sneakiest tribes in Chima. They were known for causing mischief and double-crossing. But now that they had joined the Crocs in their fight for CHI, they were also very dangerous. In fact, that was the reason Eris was in the forest right now.

I hope I'm able to find them, Eris thought. *Or else the Lions are in real trouble!*

Earlier that morning, the Ruling Council had called Eris and several other Eagles for a secret meeting. There were rumors that the Wolf Pack, led by Worriz, was hiding somewhere in the forest waiting to ambush the Lions as they distributed CHI that month. But no one knew where exactly the Wolves were hiding. It was too dangerous for the Lions to launch a scouting mission on foot. They could be easily attacked. So the Ruling Council had asked Eris and several of her fellow troops

to split up and fly above the forest to find where they were camped.

Eris had been circling for several hours now, but she hadn't spotted any sign of the Wolves. *They must be really well hidden,* she thought. *I'll never find them just by flying. I need a better plan.*

She soared over an open field that bordered the forest. Down below, a lone tree grew amidst the grass. Eris landed on a high branch and thought hard.

The Wolves might be just past the edge of the woods, watching me right now, she thought to herself. *But how do I make them show themselves? Hmm . . . Wolves like to eat . . . and howl at the moon . . . and make fun of other animals. But they don't like it when anyone makes fun of them.*

Eris smiled. That was it. She would tease the Wolves until they got so angry they would forget they were supposed to be hiding!

She looked down and realized that the tree she was sitting on was completely hollow. It was probably used by squirrels to hide their nuts in the winter. Maybe she could use it as part of her plan.

Eris flew inside the tree through a hole in the trunk. Then she turned and pushed her head back through the

hole, yelling, "Hey! Why did the Wolves cross the road? Because they were running away from the Lions!"

As soon as she said it, she ducked back into the tree. After a few moments, she poked her head back out again. "How can you tell if a Wolf is coming? Easy—by his smell!"

This time, she thought she heard a couple of growls from the woods as she dived back into the tree. When she stuck her head out of the hole a third time, she yelled extra loudly. "Stop me if you've heard this one: *Knock-knock*. Who's there? *Worriz*. Worriz who?"

Eris waited a moment, and then laughed. *"Worr-iz the best place to hide? These woods are scary!"*

Now she could hear angry grumbling coming from the forest. She puffed out her chest and made her voice as rough as she could, saying, "Look at me! I'm a Wolf. I'm the toughest animal in the forest and every other animal is afraid of me. Well, at least the mice are . . . and the ants . . . and maybe some frogs. If I see a hedgehog, I run away—but I look really tough while I'm doing it!"

That last joke did it. The Wolves came surging out of a grove of trees, growling and snapping their jaws as they charged the hollow tree. Before Eris could get out of the hole and take flight, they were all around her hiding place.

Uh-oh, thought Eris. *I found the Wolves, but now how am I supposed to get away?*

She looked all around for something that would help her escape. Then she saw them: nuts—piles and piles of nuts left by the squirrels. She scooped a bunch up in her hands and threw them out of the hole. They rained down on the Wolves, littering the ground. She tossed out more and more. The Wolves kept slipping on them and falling onto the grass. The moment they'd try to get up, they'd slip and fall down again.

Eris took advantage of the distraction and flew out through the hole in the tree, soaring high into the sky. Quickly, she raced back home to tell the Ruling Council what she had learned.

"The Wolves are camping near the trees!" she called to Ewald, the Ruling Council leader, when she arrived. "If the Lions launch an ambush now, the Wolves won't have a chance to find another hiding place. And the Lions can deliver the CHI safely."

Ewald smiled proudly at the young Eagle. "You've done well, Eris," he said. "How did you locate their hidden camp?"

Now it was Eris's turn to grin. "It was simple, in the end," she said. "My jokes drove them *nuts*!"

LONE WOLF

I t was dinnertime for the Wolf Pack. That meant three things: meat, meat, and more meat. Everyone was gathered around a large campfire and chowing down on the day's feast. All the Wolves were chomping and chewing and generally having a good time.

Everyone, that is, except Wonald.

For as far back as anyone could remember, Wonald had always been a bit . . . different. While his friends all howled at the moon, Wonald loved basking in its light. While the other Wolves snarled and growled at animals that came too near to the pack, Wonald would walk up and try to make friends.

But it was dinnertime that really set Wonald apart. His choice in food was, well, strange.

"Wonald, what *are* you doing?" A white Wolf named Windra marched up to him.

Windra was one of the most beautiful Wolves in the entire pack. She was also one of the most vicious.

Wonald gulped, then stammered, "Um, well, I'm, um . . . I'm actually making a salad."

"You're *what*?" Windra looked down at the bowl of lettuce, tomatoes, and other vegetables in front of Wondald in disgust. She took a sniff and crinkled up her nose. "That is the worst excuse for a dinner I've ever seen. Wonald, hard as it might be to believe, you are a Wolf. Wolves do not eat salad. Wolves eat *meat*."

"But I don't like meat," Wonald protested.

Windra leaned in close. "It doesn't matter if you like it or not," she hissed. "You are a *Wolf*, and it's what we *do*!"

Wonald shrugged. "Well, it's not what *I* do. Besides, if I don't have any meat, then there's more for everyone else, right?"

Windra growled in frustration and stalked away.

"Phew." Wonald exhaled. That had been close. Usually the other Wolves just ignored him when he was acting different. But tonight, they seemed especially argumentative.

When his salad was ready, Wonald went off on his own to eat. That way, he wouldn't provoke any jokes from the other Wolves, or have to watch them gulping down their dinners.

After his meal was over, Wonald returned to the rest of the pack. Even though he usually ate dinner alone, he still liked to be a part of the group. They were his family, after all. And he figured that by now they would be full from eating and would have calmed down.

Unfortunately, Wonald was wrong. All the Wolves had grown even rowdier. They were fighting amongst themselves, growling and snapping and biting.

"Stop it!" Wonald cried as he jumped away from a pair of wrestling Wolves. "Why do we have to fight all the time, just because we're Wolves?"

The others responded by snarling at him. "It's what we *do*, Wonald. If you don't like it, then maybe you shouldn't be here!"

Wonald felt hurt. He was used to being made fun of. But the others had never told him to leave. Wolves always stuck together, even when they were arguing.

Shaking his head, Wonald walked away. He decided it would be better to sleep apart from the pack tonight.

That would give them a chance to cool down. By tomorrow morning, perhaps they would be in better spirits. He headed over to a small cave where it would be quiet and dark.

Wonald slept soundly, not even stirring when there was some commotion outside. When he finally woke up, it was late the next morning. He got up, stretched, and headed for camp to see if he had any berries left for his breakfast.

But when he stepped outside, Wonald's eyes grew wide with surprise.

There was no sign of the other Wolves anywhere. All the vehicles were gone, too. It looked like the whole camp had packed up overnight and moved on somewhere else!'

"I can't believe it," he whispered. "They left me!"

Wonald's heart sank. The Wolves hadn't been just grumpy last night. They had really meant what they'd said—they had wanted Wonald to leave! And worse, they had actually moved on without him! Wolves always traveled in packs, roaming from one campsite to the next. But they never left one of their own behind . . . until now.

It must be my fault, Wonald thought sadly. *They got tired of how "different" I am and decided to kick me out of the pack. But I don't want to be on my own. I have to find them!*

Wonald sniffed the ground. Years of hunting out the tastiest nuts and berries had given him an excellent sense of smell. He could tell the pack had gone northwest. Wonald started to follow them.

After a short time, he came to a fork in the road. By the large vehicle tracks on the ground, he could tell the pack had gone right. But the wheels of their trucks had torn up all the dirt, demolishing a nearby meerkat nest.

The meerkats were busily trying to repair the damage.

Wonald walked over. "Can I help?" he asked.

"Look at this mess!" snapped one of the meerkats. "Here we had just finished cleaning up for the big family reunion—all fifteen thousand one hundred sixty-seven of our relatives are coming over!—and some nasty bunch of Wolves knocked down our house!"

"I'm sure they didn't mean it," Wonald said soothingly. "They were probably just in a hurry. Here, let me clear some of this dirt away from your holes."

The meerkats grumbled, but when they saw Wonald's large paws were better at clearing away dirt than theirs, they agreed. He had repaired the worst of the damage in no time at all.

When Wonald was done helping the meerkats rebuild their nest, he set out on the trail of the Wolves again. It wasn't long before he came upon a grove of trees that had been knocked over. A bunch of squirrels were running to and fro, gathering nuts that were scattered on the ground.

"Nuts, nuts, nuts!" said one of the squirrels.

"Yes, there are certainly a lot of them," agreed Wonald.

"No, I mean, nuts to those Wolves who knocked down our trees!" said the squirrel. "We put all our nuts in these trees, and now they're everywhere. Some are crushed. We'll never be able to recover all of them. No, no, no!"

Wonald immediately began picking up nuts and bringing them to the squirrels' pile.

As soon as the squirrels noticed him, they shook their tiny fists angrily.

"First you Wolves destroy our trees, and now you're taking our nuts!" they squeaked.

"I don't want your nuts, though they do look tasty," Wonald assured them. "I was just trying to help you clean up."

"Oh," said the squirrels. They looked sorry for yelling at him. "Well, that's all right, then. Keep going."

Once that job was finished, Wonald moved on. He couldn't believe how much damage his Wolf Pack was causing as they traveled. Sometimes he had a hard time believing he was a Wolf. He would never act this way!

The Wolves' scent was getting stronger, though, so he knew he would catch up to them any minute now.

Soon, Wonald came to a rushing river. On the shore, a little beaver was crying.

"What's the matter?" Wonald asked.

"My beautiful dam!" said the beaver. "Some Wolves came by and broke it to pieces as they crossed the river. It will take me hours to fix—and just think of all the bark I'll need to find! And the sticks and the rocks. I'll never be able to gather enough supplies. I could hire a professional dam builder, but do you know how much they cost? Five hundred pieces of tree bark an hour, and that's just for labor! And then there's—"

"It's okay," interrupted Wonald. He knew from experience that beavers would talk all day long, if given the chance. "I'll give you a paw rebuilding your dam."

Together, the Wolf and the beaver worked side by side to fix the broken dam. When they were done, the beaver offered Wonald some tree bark as a snack. Wonald said no—he wasn't *that* hungry. Besides, the scent of the Wolf pack was superstrong now. He would catch up to them any minute.

A short while later, Wonald came to a small hill. He could hear the Wolf pack on the other side, snarling and growling! Wonald ran toward the sound. Just as he reached the top of the hill, he spotted them. Windra and the other Wolves were chasing some rabbits away from

their grazing ground. And the wheels from their huge trucks were completely ripping up the grass as they went.

"Hey! Stop!" Wonald cried, rushing forward. "Leave the rabbits alone!"

"What are you going to do about it?" growled one of the Wolves, without turning around. "Get lost!"

"That's what you told me the last time," Wonald said. "And I spent all day trying to find you again. But after seeing all the damage the pack has done and the way you've ruined so many innocent animals' homes, I'm not sure I want to be with you guys after all."

The Wolf who had snapped at Wonald suddenly looked over his shoulder. His eyes widened and his jaw dropped. "It's Wonald! Hey, everybody, it's Wonald!"

The rest of the Wolves turned.

"Wonald? Where?"

"Did someone say *Wonald*?"

"Out of the way, let me see!"

The whole pack suddenly surrounded the young Wolf. Even the rabbits stopped running and watched what was happening, puzzled. Wonald didn't know what it all meant, either.

"Why are you guys so happy to see me?" he asked. "You're the ones who ran off and left me, remember?"

"*We* didn't abandon *you*," Windra said, running up to him. "*You* abandoned *us*. When it was time to move out, you were nowhere to be found."

"I didn't know you were leaving!" Wonald insisted.

"Worriz told us right after supper," said one of the Wolves. "Didn't you hear him? We spent the entire evening packing up camp."

Wonald suddenly remembered that he had walked out after supper. He had missed the pack leader's speech to the other Wolves. That was why he didn't know the pack was traveling on before dawn.

"We looked everywhere, but couldn't find you," said Windra.

"I came looking for you, but only saw all the damage you have been doing in the forest," answered Wonald.

"Well, we were upset," said an older Wolf. "We thought you had deserted the pack. No one has *ever* left the pack. You might not always act like we do, but you are still one of us, Wonald."

Hearing that the other Wolves had missed him made Wonald happier than he'd been all day. Still, he couldn't shake aside his disappointment at the destruction the Wolves had caused.

"I know you were upset," he said. "But you guys caused a lot of damage to other animals today. I'm not sure I'm ready to rejoin the pack just yet."

All the Wolves gasped.

"You really would leave us?" they cried in dismay.

"Well," said Wonald slowly. He looked over at the rabbits crouched nearby. The little bunnies were still shaking in fear, but they were mostly stunned by what was happening.

"I've been helping the animals repair everything you guys destroyed today," Wonald said. "I think I could be convinced to rejoin the pack, *if* we helped the rabbits clean up their grazing field."

"If we *what*?" many of the Wolves exclaimed. They didn't like being told what to do, especially if it involved helping.

But the elder Wolf quieted them. "Wonald is one of us," he said in a loud voice. "So perhaps, just this one time, we should try things his way." The older Wolf then looked over to Worriz for approval. Growling, Worriz nodded in agreement.

The pack spent a short while helping repair the damage to the grass while the rabbits watched on in amazement. The little creatures kept their distance. But they seemed rooted to the spot. They had never seen the Wolves being *helpful* before!

When the Wolves had finished, the grass looked better . . . mostly. Wonald smiled. It would do.

"All right, enough helping," snapped Windra. "Wonald's back. So we had better find a new place to camp for the night. Preferably where there are plenty of"—She gave Wonald a long look—"*vegetables*," she said through gritted teeth.

Wonald grinned.

That night, he had his usual salad for dinner. But this time, when the others went to howl at the moon, Wonald went with them. He still thought it was kind of a silly thing to do, but they were his family after all.

Together, the Wolves howled happily until the dawn.

WORRIZ'S CHALLENGE

Eris perched on a rock and gazed down at the ground far below, her brow knitted with concern. Just as she had for the last six days, she could see Wolves prowling at the base of the cliffs that the Eagles called home. Now and then, one of the Wolves would look up at her, flash a savage grin, and give a short howl. She did her best to ignore the taunts. But this was becoming a concern.

Ever since the battle for CHI had begun among the tribes, the Wolves had been encroaching on Eagle territory. Normally, the Wolf pack was constantly on the move. But this pack was acting like they were here to stay. They were noisy, messy, and threw loud parties late into the night so that none of the Eagles could sleep.

It might have just been a little inconvenience, except for two things: One, the Eagles needed to be able to fly down to the ground to find food, and the Wolves were making that dangerous to do. And two, it was almost time for the Eagles to get their monthly share of the powerful CHI from the Lions, and Eris was sure the Wolves were here to prevent that from happening.

If only we could find some way to make them go away, she thought. *But how?*

Just then, Eglor flew by. He was very excited, and kept shouting, "I've done it! I've done it!" All the Wolves looked up to see what the commotion was about.

"Shhhh!" warned Eris. "What have you done?"

But Eglor was too excited to speak quietly. "I've perfected a machine that can hurl an Eagle all the way from one end of the forest to the other, faster than any beast that runs or flies. From now on, instead of *flap, flap, flap* to get from one place to another, it will be *zip, zip, zip!*"

"*Zip, zip, zip?*" said one of the Wolves, laughing. "Sounds more like *flop, flop, flop* to me!"

Eglor wheeled in the air and looked down at the Wolf. "*Ha!* With my machine, any Eagle could outrace a Wolf by twice the speed. That's just scientific fact. There's not even the teeniest, tiniest, most microscopic room for doubt."

"Want to bet?" growled Worriz. The pack leader had wandered over to see what the rest of the Wolves were so interested in. Now he eyed Eglor with a mocking smile.

"Eglor, don't." Eris tried to hold her friend back.

"No good can come from arguing with the Wolves."

But Eglor's pride as an inventor was at stake now. "Yes, I do want to bet!" he announced loudly.

"All right, then," said Worriz. "I'll bet you I can make it to the far end of the woods faster than any Eagle launched from your machine. If I win, you Eagles give up your share of CHI to us this month."

"And if you *lose*," said Eglor, "you go away and leave our nesting area alone!"

Eris slapped a wing against her forehead. What had Eglor just gotten them into?

"Deal," said Worriz. "We race tomorrow . . . That is, if you can find someone foolish enough to challenge me."

"Tomorrow?" stammered Eglor. He suddenly sounded

a bit nervous. "Now, see here, the machine works—I know it does—but it hasn't been fully tested yet, and there are still a few things—"

The Wolves howled with laughter. One of them said, "You know what they say about Eagles—all flash and feathers."

"If you want to back down, bird," Worriz sneered, "then I guess—"

"I'll do it!" Eris interrupted him. "I'll race you!"

After she had said it, she could hardly believe the words had come out of her beak. But the Wolves were getting under her feathers with all their insults, and maybe this was the one way to get them to leave their nesting grounds for good. Besides, Eglor was a great inventor. If he said his machine could make her go *zip, zip, zip,* then it could.

"All right then," Worriz snarled. "Tomorrow. Dawn. Be here."

The Wolves turned to talk amongst themselves. Suddenly, Worriz looked sharply back up at Eris. "Oh, and one more rule," he snapped. "No help from the Lions, right, Eagle? For this challenge, you fly solo."

All the Wolves laughed.

🐺 🐺 🐺 🐺 🐺

"It doesn't work," said Eglor sadly. "I don't know what happened, but it's not working."

"What do you mean?" asked Eris, in shock. "You told the Wolves there wasn't the teeniest, tiniest room for doubt."

It was the middle of the night. Eglor had taken Eris to see his machine, which consisted of a catapult with a bowl at the end attached to a much bigger metal apparatus by tightly wound springs. When Eglor triggered the contraption, the bowl would be propelled forward and anything inside it would go flying . . . at least, in theory.

But now the inventor Eagle didn't look so sure.

"When I tested it this afternoon, it worked fine," Eglor explained. "But then I started practicing tonight with things actually in the bowl, like bunches of apples, and . . . well, look for yourself."

Eris looked. There were smashed apples splattered all over the floor of Eglor's workshop. The machine just hurled them straight down at the ground.

"So if I get in this thing tomorrow morning . . . no *zip*?" she asked.

"More like *splat*," said Eglor. "We'll have to call off the bet."

"We can't," insisted Eris. "We'll lose our CHI to the Wolves, which will hurt the balance in Chima, and the Wolves will stay down there forever! I have to win the race . . . somehow. I just have to."

"Did you do it?" whispered Worriz.

Wilhurt, another Wolf in the pack, nodded. "It was easy. I used a bellow plant to float up the mountain and then tied it down. I got to Eglor's workshop, and broke off part of his machine. Then I let the air out of the bellow plant little by little so I could float back down. That Eagle won't be zipping anywhere, boss."

"Good," Worriz said with a wicked grin. "All that Eagle CHI is practically ours. Hey, maybe we'll challenge the Bears and the Gorillas to races, too. Let the Crocs fight battles—we'll get all the CHI we want the old-fashioned way: We'll cheat."

By dawn, Eris had a plan . . . sort of. It started with *not* telling Worriz the machine didn't work. The second part involved getting some help from someone she would normally stay far away from.

Skinnit the Skunk was actually a very nice animal who didn't have an enemy in the world. But no one really wanted to spend any time around him because . . . well, he smelled really bad. It wasn't his fault. But no one wanted to risk keeping him company and maybe winding up smelling terribly, too. Still, Eris had always made an effort to be polite to him.

"Skinnit, can you do me a favor?" she asked, talking to him from high up in a tree.

"*Me?* Really? You want me to do you a favor?" Skinnit replied eagerly. No one ever asked him to do anything other than go away.

"That's right," said Eris. "It's nothing hard. I just want you to do . . . that thing you do at a certain place and a certain time."

Skinnit frowned. "You mean you want me to make a stink?" he asked. That was what he did best, but it always made other animals run away. Why would Eris want him to do that?

"Just trust me," Eris reassured him. "You'll be doing something nice for all the Eagles."

"If you say so," Skinnit answered, smiling. "But you had better hold your beak—it's going to get smelly around here!"

Eris grinned. "Thanks, Skinnit," she said. "I knew I could count on you." With that, she flew off. She had a few more non-rule-breaking favors to ask of some old friends.

After making a few more stops, Eris was ready for the start of the race. She perched in Eglor's lab, waiting for the signal to start. Down below, Worriz was crouched down, ready to run.

"You might as well hand over that CHI now, bird," Worriz called up. "It's as good as ours!"

"We'll just see about that," Eris shouted back down. She glanced over at Eglor, and gave him a wink. The inventor Eagle looked very nervous, but he nodded back.

One of the Wolves stood at the base of the rock spire, holding a palm leaf to start the race. A moment later, he waved the leaf high in the air, and the race was on!

Eris leaped out from Eglor's lab, flying as fast as she could, so anyone looking from below would think she had been rocketed out into the sky. Worriz was running at top speed, too, hoping to put some distance between himself and the Eagle.

As she soared above the canopy of trees, Eris did her best to keep an eye on Worriz, even if she could only see him for a few seconds now and then. She knew the Wolf

would take the fastest path through the forest. In fact, she was counting on it.

In the woods, Worriz was feeling confident. The pack had blazed a new trail through the forest lately, one that made getting from one end to the other a snap. All he had to do was follow the scent the vehicles had left and he couldn't go wrong. He put his nose to the ground, took a big sniff . . .

. . . and he almost fell over! His nose was full of an incredibly horrible smell, so bad it made his eyes water. He shook his head, trying to make the odor go away. But it didn't. It was so overpowering that now he couldn't smell anything else. Worriz knew there was only one animal in the forest who could make a smell that bad.

"Skinnit!" he howled.

Off to the side of the path, the little skunk ran away, disappearing into the trees.

"All right, I don't need my nose," Worriz

grumbled to himself. "I can remember the path . . . sort of. I know there were trees . . . and a big rock . . . and some dirt . . . hmm . . ."

Worriz picked a direction that looked right and started to run again. At one point, he glanced up and spotted Eris through the trees. The Eagle was falling behind. All he needed to do was put on an extra burst of speed and he was sure to win.

Just then, he heard an enormous rustling in the woods ahead. It sounded like a huge herd of creatures on the move. But there were no sounds of foliage tearing or ground being ripped up the way he would have expected. As he rounded a bend, he discovered why: It was a tribe of Gorillas in their massive Gorilla Machines. But instead of smashing through the jungle the way the Wolf Vehicles did, the Gorillas were being extra careful not to disturb anything as they passed.

The Gorillas' respect for nature meant that they had to move very slowly in their huge machines so they didn't accidentally trample any flowers or even weeds.

"Come on!" Worriz growled. "Hurry it up!"

Three of the Gorillas stopped right in Worriz's path. "Hey, Wolf, why are you in such a hurry?" said the first Gorilla, looking down from the cockpit of his huge vehicle.

"Yeah, you have to savor every minute of life, the way you do a really good banana," said the second.

"Maybe you just don't see it," said the third. "You Wolves always have your noses to the ground, and you don't look up to see the sky!"

Over Worriz's protests, the Gorillas proceeded to tell him all about how much better life was when you were in tune with all of nature. Even worse, all the other Gorillas stopped to listen, nodding their heads and smiling. It felt like forever before they finally finished and moved on, their machines going even slower than before.

When the Gorillas had finally passed, Worriz ran faster than he ever had in his life. He was heading for

the quick-moving river that flowed through this part of the forest. If he dove in and let the waters carry him, he could still beat Eris. Sure, he wouldn't technically be racing. But so what? The only thing that mattered to him was winning!

He was just about to dive into the river when, from behind the trees, a bunch of small figures appeared in his path. Worriz nearly skidded to a halt. He couldn't believe his eyes. Nearly two dozen teenage foxes were blocking him, all smiling and yipping and jumping up and down. Because as everyone in Chima knew, teenage foxes thought that the Wolves were the *coolest* animals in the forest. Especially the Wolf Pack leader, Worriz.

"Look, it's Worriz!" cried one.

"I told you he was coming!" squealed another.

"Wow, look how cool he is!"

"I just *have* to get his autograph! I have to!"

Before Worriz knew what was happening, he was being mobbed by the teenage foxes! They were tugging at his fur, running back and forth in front of him, and begging for his signature.

"We're your biggest fans," said one of the foxes breathlessly. "You're the *coolest* Wolf in Chima!"

"Could you howl for us? Please, please, *please!*" begged another.

"Get out of my way!" roared Worriz.

But the foxes wouldn't move. They clung to his arms and kept trying to hand him sheets of paper and pencils for his autograph. Worriz had to elbow his way past them, and even then, they wouldn't stop chasing after him. They followed him all the way to the edge of the woods, only leaving when he emerged onto a field where Eris was waiting for him.

"I won," said the Eagle. "So pack up your pack and move on."

But Worriz sneered. *"Ha!"* he said. "That's what you think. Your Lion pals aren't here, so you can't prove you won the race. Looks like your CHI for this month is ours. Hand it over!"

Eris shook her head, a knowing grin crossing her face. She pointed up at the sky. A whole flock of sparrows was circling overhead, cheering wildly for Eris.

"I don't need the Lions to prove I beat you," she said. "Those sparrows saw the entire race. It's over, Worriz."

Worriz smacked his head and groaned. Even with cheating, he had still lost to the Eagles! "Fine," he grumbled. "You got lucky this time. But next time, mark my words, you won't be so lucky!"

Eris chuckled. "It wasn't luck," she said as a sparrow came and landed on her hand. "Don't you know by now? I have lots of friends."

TABLE OF CONTENTS

FIGHTING FOR CHIMA

Welcome to the land of Chima. For hundreds of years, this kingdom was a peaceful place. But that was before the great conflict. Now a fierce battle rages on, turning friends into enemies and pitting tribe against tribe. We have rebuilt our vehicles to use them as fighting machines. The woods, plains, and jungles are places of peril. Chima has become a battlefield.

One thing, though, has not changed. The CHI—Chima's most precious energy source. We Lions continue to collect CHI Orbs in the Sacred Pool. Once a month, we share the CHI evenly among all the tribes despite the battles we fight. CHI must be used equally; otherwise untold calamities will befall Chima.

I am LaGravis, the king of the Lions. My tribe guards the CHI against the devious attacks of the Crocodiles, Wolves, and Ravens. We will defend our world and its ancient traditions no matter what it takes. But we could not do it without the powerful help of our allies.

The Gorillas are possibly the strongest and most agile warriors in Chima. If they wanted, they could easily defeat just about any other tribe in the land. However, they are not warriors by nature. They prefer to live in harmony with the world and spend hours each day meditating in a state they call "the Great Mellow."

The peaceful members of this tribe live in the jungle treetops, swinging from branch to branch and admiring all of nature's wonders. A Gorilla could pass an entire afternoon watching a flower grow.

But when the safety of Chima is threatened, Gorillas will do everything they can to protect the land they love. Using their incredible strength and lightning-fast reflexes, Gorillas can defeat even the most experienced warriors. And their battle machines are modeled after their own bodies, capable of pummeling an entire army in seconds. We Lions are very lucky to have the Gorillas at our side.

Despite his intimidating appearance, Gorzan the Gorilla is actually one of the most soft-hearted creatures in Chima. He is incredibly powerful and can defeat an enemy in seconds, but he will later anguish over "the poor plants" he stepped on during the battle.

Gorzan is extremely sensitive and spends most of his time watching flowers. He sometimes feels another creature's pain before they even realize they *had* any pain. And his favorite way to greet everyone is with a big bear hug. Gorzan is close friends with my son, Laval. He was once friends with Cragger the Crocodile Prince, too. That is, until Cragger turned vicious in his quest to control all the CHI. Gorzan's warrior instincts kick in the moment someone threatens one of his friends . . . or tramples his favorite flowers.

LaGravis says:

Though Gorzan fights to protect Chima from the Crocs, Wolves, and Ravens, he still believes there is good in every animal, including his enemies.

THE RAVENS

The Ravens are a very sneaky tribe. They are also one of the greediest in Chima. These sharp-tongued thieves can't keep themselves from stealing, regardless of the value of the things they suddenly decide to "take care of." Being on friendly terms with the Ravens doesn't help—they steal as much from their friends as from their enemies.

They will be more than happy to sell someone back their missing item at a "fair price." If you're lucky, you may even get a discount! That's how the Ravens make a deal. No amount of arguing will get a Raven to admit he's stolen your property—in fact, he'll insist he's giving you a break by offering it for half price!

But don't underestimate these crafty birds' fighting abilities. They can be vicious opponents, especially if there's a profit to be turned. Greed for reward is the only reason the Raven Tribe has allied with the Crocodiles in their fight for the CHI.

Razar the Raven has swindled every single member of his tribe at least once—and they all respect him greatly for it. After all, Razar is a keen follower of his family's traditions: His parents sold him more than seventeen times (and then stole him back, so they could sell him again).

Razar has a metal hook in place of one hand. No one knows how he lost it . . . perhaps he just traded it. Razar loves wheeling, dealing, and stealing. And no matter what, he'll insist he's "cutting you a deal!"

Razar never does anything that doesn't somehow benefit him. That's why he had the Raven Tribe join with Cragger in the battle for CHI. He's certain he can turn a profit when the dust settles. Razar is a pure mercenary who will fight for the highest bidder . . . and then steal all their weapons while they're not looking.

LaGravis says:

Unlike Cragger, Razar would rather steal trinkets and treasures than CHI. It's easier to turn a profit!

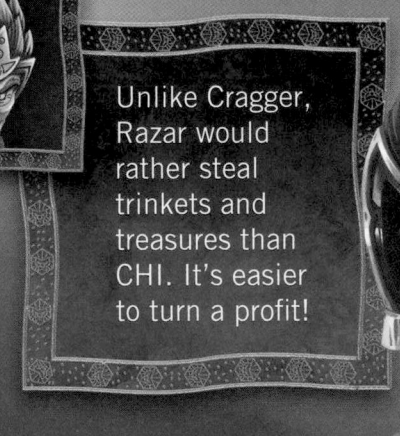

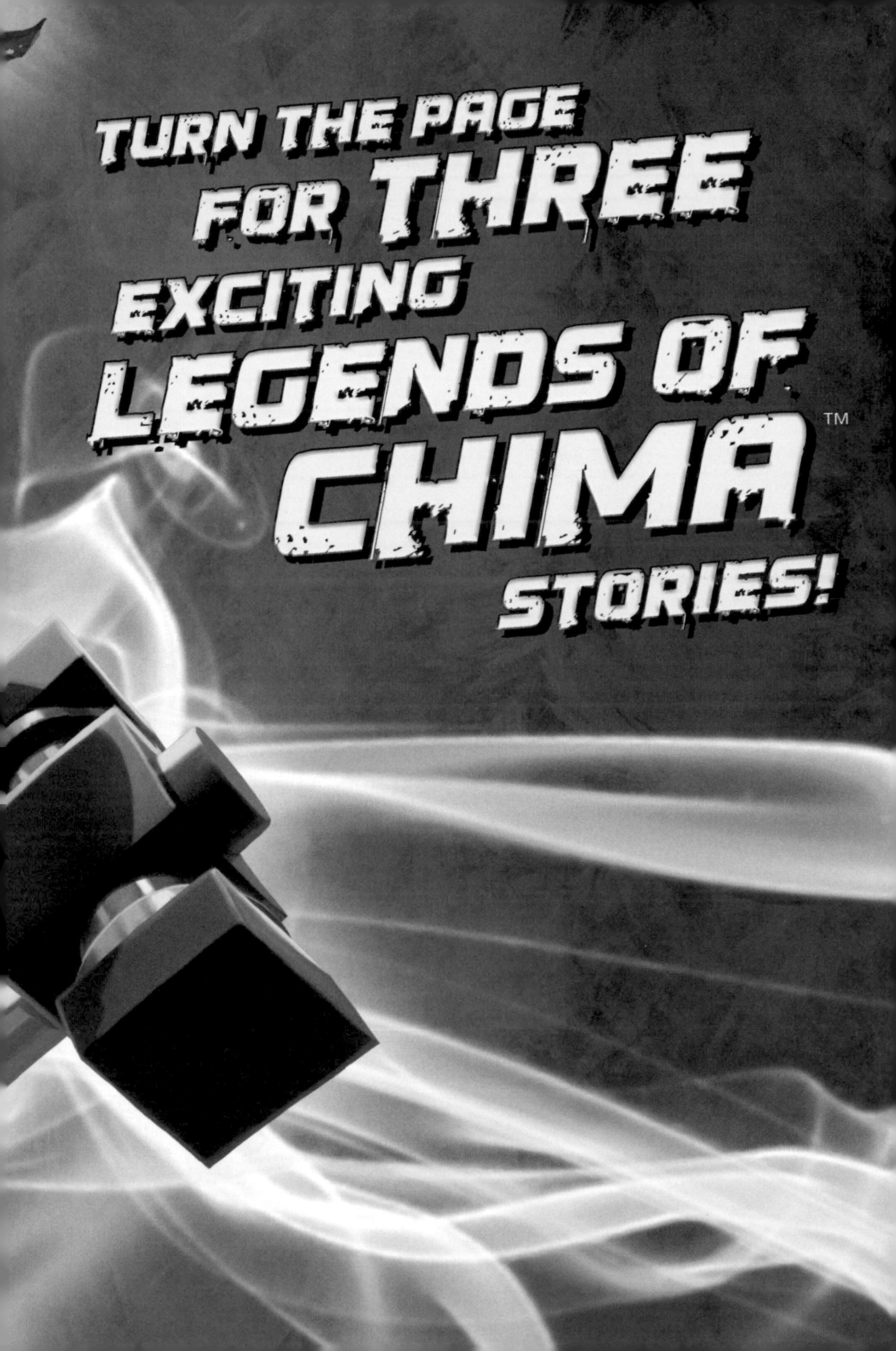
TURN THE PAGE FOR THREE EXCITING LEGENDS OF CHIMA™ STORIES!

A GROOVY DAY

It was a warm, sunny morning in Chima. Gorzan the Gorilla smiled as he headed up a steep rocky path along one of Chima's tallest mountains. Little did he know, danger lurked directly behind him.

This is too easy, thought Wilhurt the Wolf as he followed Gorzan. *That foolish Gorilla is going to lead me right to his hidden stash of CHI!*

Earlier that morning, Wilhurt had heard a rumor among the Wolf Pack that the Gorillas were hiding a large stockpile of CHI in a new secret location. Then, Wilhurt spotted Gorzan walking through the forest. He realized this was his chance. Surely the Gorilla was heading straight to check on the new hiding place of the CHI!

All I have to do is follow him, and their CHI is ours, Wilhurt thought with a wicked grin.

Quietly, the Wolf trailed Gorzan. He made sure to keep his distance but always had the Gorilla in sight. Wilhurt climbed farther and farther up the mountain, following Gorzan until they reached a narrow ledge. Suddenly, a giant boulder fell directly behind them!

The ground shook as the rock smashed onto the trail. The path back down the mountain was completely blocked.

"Whoa!" exclaimed Wilhurt, jumping clear. Then he gasped. He'd just given himself away.

To Wilhurt's surprise, Gorzan slowly turned and smiled brightly at him.

"Oh, hey there, Wolf-*dude*," Gorzan said. "Didn't see you there. Great view, huh?"

"Great . . . what?" Wilhurt stammered.

"From up here, you can see *all* of Chima." Gorzan held his arms out wide. "Times like this, you really feel one with the Great Mellow, you know?"

"The great . . . *what*?" sputtered Wilhurt. Then he growled. "Enough messing around, Gorilla. Show me where your hidden CHI stash is!"

Gorzan shook his head, still smiling. "Aw, come on; take a little time to relax. Enjoy the fresh air. Be one with the Great Mellow. You know, we Gorillas have a saying . . ."

Gorzan then proceeded to explain at length the Gorilla Tribe's philosophy about nature, harmony, and the meaning of life in general.

The next three hours did not go well for Wilhurt. No matter how hard he tried, he couldn't get Gorzan to reveal the secret location of the CHI. The Gorilla just kept going on and on about how all the animals in Chima were "brothers and sisters" to one another, under their fur . . . or feathers . . . or scales. The more Wilhurt snarled and snapped, the more Gorzan talked about peace, love, and understanding.

As the sun sank lower in the sky, Wilhurt couldn't take it anymore. He was trapped on a ledge with a Gorilla who wouldn't stop talking, and it was driving him crazy.

I don't care about the CHI at this point, he thought desperately. *I just need to get past that boulder and*

down the mountain. Or make that Gorilla stop talking. Wilhurt glanced over the side of the ledge. The soft, leafy treetops weren't that far below them. *What if I give him a little push?* Wilhurt thought. *He'll land on the trees below. He'll be fine. Gorillas do it all the time. And then I'll finally have some silence!*

"Hey, look, down there," Wilhurt said. "I see, um, a Lion and a Crocodile hugging!"

Gorzan beamed. "Where? Where?" he asked, leaning forward.

Quickly, Wilhurt ran at Gorzan and pushed with all his might. But the Gorilla was so big and strong that he never even felt Wilhurt's shoves.

"Can't see it, but it must have been a sight." Gorzan sighed. "Hey, maybe we should hug, too, Wilhurt!"

"Uh . . . sure thing," Wilhurt replied, already hatching a plan. When Gorzan turned to him, arms outstretched, Wilhurt threw himself at the Gorilla, intending to knock him off the ledge. Instead, Wilhurt just bounced right off.

Gorzan laughed. "Is that how you hug in the Wolf Pack? I've never seen that before, but there's room in the Great Mellow for all kinds of new things. Why, just the other day, I was saying, 'I bet the Wolves aren't as bad as everyone thinks. They just need somebody to hold out a paw.' Right?"

"Yeah, right," growled Wilhurt. He was starting to get a headache. He didn't know how much longer he could take of this. "You know, we might get a better view from up higher," Wilhurt suggested. "Why don't you climb up, and then you can reach down and pull me after you. Right, um . . . er . . . brother?"

Gorzan's face lit up. "That's a great idea!" he exclaimed.

Wilhurt chuckled. He thought it was a great idea, too. Since the rock face above them was almost sheer, Gorzan was sure to slip and fall if he tried to climb it.

Gorzan made a good effort, but there were hardly any handholds. Twice, he almost lost his grip and tumbled off the mountain. But both times he caught himself before he fell.

"Maybe I can . . . give you a boost?" Wilhurt suggested. He grabbed one of Gorzan's legs and tugged with all his might, hoping to pull the Gorilla off the mountain. To his surprise, Gorzan started laughing. Then Gorzan kicked out his leg, slamming Wilhurt into the rocks alongside the path.

"Sorry, brother," Gorzan apologized. "I'm ticklish there."

By now, Wilhurt was really desperate. He peered back over the ledge. *The trees aren't that far away*, he thought. *I think I can make it if I jump. All I know is I can't stay up here with this Gorilla one more second!*

Taking a deep breath, Wilhurt jumped.

"Owww! Ouch! *Owoo!*" Wilhurt howled loudly as he bounced off the mountain and crashed through the tree leaves. He hit the ground with an "Oof!" and lay still. He had made it. He was off the mountain. And away from the Gorilla.

Wilhurt was just breathing a sigh of relief when, suddenly, there was Gorzan swinging easily down through the trees to land beside him.

"Hey, Wolf-dude!" Gorzan called. "Cool jump. You just trusted yourself to nature, huh? That's the best way to be one with the Great Mellow."

"Wait a minute!" shouted Wilhurt. "How did you get down here so fast? We were trapped up there!"

"Trapped?" Gorzan asked, scratching his head. "I wasn't trapped. I go up there all the time. I just took the shortcut to get down."

Wilhurt thought his head would explode. "Then why didn't you say we could get down? We've been up there the entire day!"

"I know." Gorzan smiled. "It was awesome, wasn't it? We should do this all the time. You know, the Great Mellow has a saying . . ."

Wilhurt got to his feet and ran through the jungle as fast as he could. He zipped past trees and through bushes—anything to get as far away as possible from the sound of Gorzan's voice. When he finally thought he was safe, he paused to take a breath.

But to his dismay, not far in the distance, he could hear Gorzan echoing after him. "Hey, Wilhurt! *Willllhurt!* Come back! I think somebody needs a *huuuuuuug*!"

BASIC TRAINING

It was afternoon at the Lion Camp. Laval, the Lion Prince, paced back and forth, very, very frustrated. "I can't believe the Gorillas," he muttered to himself. "They just do whatever they want!"

Earlier that morning, Laval and a small group of Lion Troops had delivered CHI to the Gorilla Tribe. Just as they had reached the camp, a band of Crocs

attacked them! Laval had ordered his troops into battle formations, but the Gorillas . . . well, they had kind of done their own thing. When Laval told them to charge, they swung through the trees. When Laval tossed them CHI Orbs, they missed catching them and dropped bananas on the Crocs' heads instead.

We were lucky to beat the Crocs at all with the way they fought, Laval thought bitterly. *And next time, we might not be so lucky. It could be worse than just a single battle. We could lose control of all of the CHI in Chima!*

Laval was still pacing angrily when his father, King LaGravis, put a hand on his shoulder. "What's the matter, Son?" he asked. "You seem worried."

"It's the Gorillas," Laval answered. "They just . . . they won't listen!"

"Listen to what?" LaGravis frowned.

"Every time we go into a fight with the Crocodiles and the Wolves, the Gorillas just do whatever they like," Laval complained. "I give them orders, but they do the exact opposite. You never know where they will be on the battlefield at any moment, or what they will be doing. They have no discipline!"

LaGravis smiled. Here was his son, the reckless and headstrong Lion Prince, complaining about someone else acting the same way. *Maybe*, he thought, *this would be a good time for Laval to learn a lesson.*

"You know, you're right," LaGravis said. "Someone needs to teach them how to march and drill and fight as a unit."

Laval nodded eagerly. "Exactly! I figured I would ask Longtooth to do it. He has a lot of experience, and—"

"No," LaGravis said, shaking his head. "I need Longtooth here. You should train them, Laval."

"Me?" Laval replied, shocked. "But I . . ."

"The Gorillas trust you," LaGravis said firmly. "You are the only Lion that can train them properly."

"I guess so," Laval said slowly. Then he squared his shoulders. "All right, Dad. I'll do it. I'll train the Gorillas. You can count on me."

"I know I can, Son," LaGravis replied. As he walked away, a small grin crossed the king's face. This was going to be an important lesson for the young Lion Prince.

"You want to teach us something?" Gorzan said. He was hanging upside down on a tree branch, his eyes closed. He had been meditating on the nature of the Great Mellow when Laval showed up.

"That's right," Laval said. "I want you and the other Gorillas to show up tomorrow morning at the big field just south of the creek. We'll start training then."

"Gorillas just love to learn new things," Gorzan answered. "It's all part of the big tapestry that is life in Chima."

"Yeah, sure," Laval replied quickly. "Just remember, tomorrow morning."

The next day, Laval arrived at the field to find a small group of Gorillas waiting for him. But it wasn't all of the fighters from the tribe. And the ones who had shown up weren't exactly ready for training. Some were lying in the grass at the edge of the field. Others were sniffing flowers or pointing up at the clouds.

"Gorzan, where is everyone?" Laval asked, annoyed. "This is important. Everyone needs to be here."

"It wasn't the right time for some of the brothers," Gorzan answered. "They have other roles to play in the Great Mellow, at least until lunch. But we're all ready to learn whatever you want to teach us."

"All right." Laval sighed. He could tell this wasn't going to be easy. "We'll just have to make do. Everybody, on your feet."

One by one, the Gorillas stood up. They didn't seem in any particular hurry. Some stretched, others grabbed fruit from nearby branches. A few even started singing.

"Quiet!" Laval ordered. "Now pay attention. We're going to start with drills. Everyone get into a line."

About three-quarters of the Gorillas got into a straight line. The rest formed a crazy, sort of zigzag pattern.

"What are they doing?" Laval asked.

"They're making a line," Gorzan said.

"That's not a line," Laval said. "That's a zigzag."

"To you, maybe." Gorzan smiled. "But to them, that's what a line looks like."

Laval smacked his head. "That doesn't make sense. Everyone knows what a line looks like!"

"There's room in the Great Mellow for all sorts of lines," Gorzan said. A few of the other Gorillas nodded their heads.

Laval sighed. "Okay, fine. Everyone form a . . . mellow line. Now when I say 'turn left,' everybody turn left. Understand?"

The Gorillas nodded.

"Turn left!" Laval ordered.

Half the Gorillas turned left. The other half turned to the right.

"No, no!" Laval burst out. "Left. I said left!"

"But we did turn left," Gorzan insisted.

Laval groaned. "Don't you guys even know your left from your right?"

Gorzan walked up to Laval and put his hand on his shoulder. "Brother, turn to your left, then back to face me."

Laval did as he was asked. When he was looking at Gorzan again, the Gorilla said, "Now what did you see?"

"The big bush near the creek," Laval answered.

"Good. Now this time, turn your back to me."

When Laval had done so, Gorzan said, "Turn to your left again."

Laval turned. Now he saw the fruit trees that dotted the big, open field.

"You turned left twice, Laval," Gorzan explained, "and both times you faced in a different direction and saw a different part of the world. But which turn was truly to the left?"

Laval clenched his teeth. He knew the Gorillas meant well. But the battlefield was no place for philosophy or open interpretation. The battlefield needed discipline and order!

"Fine," Laval said. "Let's try a different approach."

"What will you teach us now?" Gorzan asked brightly.

Laval turned to face the big Gorilla and went into a battle stance. "Pretend I'm a Crocodile out to steal your CHI. Now stop me!"

"Oh, good. A game." Gorzan grinned.

Laval, for his part, had this all figured out. *The moment he charges, I'll duck out of the way*, he thought. *Then I'll grab Gorzan's arm and use the leverage to send him flying. This will impress the other Gorillas so much that they'll want to listen to me!*

Gorzan charged. Laval sidestepped, grabbed the Gorilla's arm, and pulled. But to his surprise, Gorzan didn't budge. He pulled some more. After a few minutes, he tried pushing. Gorzan didn't move an inch.

"I think I won," Gorzan pointed out.

Laval sat down on a rock and put his chin in his hands. This was getting him nowhere. The Gorillas just didn't understand the importance of learning basic tactics to fight their enemies.

But I promised Dad, Laval thought. *So no matter what, I have to train the Gorillas! Somehow.*

"Okay, next exercise," Laval said, determined.

"Suppose there are Crocs hiding in the creek back there. You need to sneak up and surprise them, and then—"

"Sneak?" asked one of the Gorillas.

"You know, sneak," Laval said. "Get down on your bellies and crawl along the ground so you can't be seen."

Laval had never seen so many shocked expressions at one time before. One of the larger Gorillas raised his hand. "Um, we can't do that," he said. "We would be crushing all the grass and flowers. Besides, Gorillas don't sneak."

"Why not?" Laval asked impatiently.

Gorzan picked up a large, fallen tree branch off the ground and snapped it in half. The two pieces landed at his feet with a loud *thunk*. "We don't need to," he said happily.

Laval looked down at the ground and counted to ten. His father had once told him it was a good way to keep his temper under control. In this case, he ended up having to count to one hundred.

"Fine, let's try a battle simulation with no sneaking," Laval said finally. "I will go hide. You try to find me. It will be good practice for tracking down Croc Spies. Close your eyes and count to . . . whatever number you guys want to count to."

The Gorillas dutifully closed their eyes. Laval ran off toward the creek and hid in the high grass. Five minutes

went by, then ten, then twenty, with no sign of the Gorillas. Finally, Laval poked his head above the grass to see what was happening.

To his dismay, the Gorillas were relaxing again. Laval sprang up and stomped over to them.

"You were supposed to come and look for me!" he cried.

"And we were going to," Gorzan replied. "But then we remembered that, in the Great Mellow, everyone ends up in the place they were meant to be. We didn't want to take you away from where you were, if you were happy there."

"But I wasn't—" Laval exploded angrily. Then he caught himself and calmed his voice. "Okay. Here's something easy. Get together—no, it doesn't have to be in a line—and walk across the field. That's all. Just walk. Can you do that?"

Gorzan looked at the field, then back at Laval. "I don't think so."

"Why not?" cried Laval. "It's simple! Anyone can do it. Look, watch me."

"Laval, I really wouldn't do that—" Gorzan began.

"I know, I know." Laval threw his arms up in the air. "I'll trample the flowers, or the Great Mellow wants me to march across some other field miles away from here. Well, I'm going, and you can follow me like warriors or stay here and look at clouds some more."

Before anyone could reply, Laval marched into the field. He was about halfway across when there was a loud *snap*. He looked down to see that his foot was caught in a wooden trap, the kind the Crocodiles sometimes put around the swamp to catch trespassers. It didn't hurt, but it was clamped tight. Laval couldn't get himself free from the snare.

He could have called for help, of course. But after ignoring Gorzan's advice, he would look like a fool if he admitted he had walked right into a trap. Instead, he pretended to be admiring the scenery while he struggled to wrench his foot loose.

After a few minutes, Gorzan asked, "Why have you stopped?"

"Oh, I just . . . thought I'd see what all the fuss was over these flowers," Laval answered, trying to sound like nothing unusual was happening. "I might, um, stay here for a while."

Gorzan looked at the other Gorillas. He didn't have to say a word. They all knew what to do.

In one fluid motion, three Gorillas swung up into the trees. They moved swiftly along the branches, passing from limb to limb. Finally, they reached the place where Laval was trapped. Moving like clockwork, one Gorilla

dropped to the ground while the other two formed a chain from the branch above. The first Gorilla used his massive strength to pry open the trap, while the one hanging from the tree scooped Laval up into the air. The whole rescue mission took less than thirty seconds.

Laval watched, amazed. He had seen the Gorillas in battle and knew they could fight. But he had never seen them in this kind of action. Without an order being given, they acted like a well-trained squad.

Once Laval was back with the Gorillas, he turned to Gorzan. "That was amazing," he said in awe. "If you can do that, why couldn't you do the things I was asking you to do before?"

"We could have," Gorzan admitted. "But we aren't Lions, Laval. We have our own way of doing things. We listen to the wind, the grass, and our own instincts rather than orders. And you should have listened to us. We knew the Crocodiles had been busy in that field. That could only mean trouble."

Laval thought about what Gorzan was saying.

He had been trying to get the Gorillas to train in the same way Lions did. *Maybe I was just getting frustrated with the Gorillas on the battlefield because they don't fight like Lions do*, he thought. *But it looks like their fighting style is just fine as it is.*

"I came to teach you," Laval said, smiling, "but I think I'm the one who ended up learning something."

"Then maybe we can teach you something else," Gorzan said, his face brightening. "Have you ever looked at clouds? Watched them for a whole afternoon? That one up there looks like Cragger. . . ."

Laval spent the rest of the day with the Gorillas, lying in the grass, just looking up at the sky.

THE AUCTION

"Holy Razoli, I must be seeing things!" Rizzo the Raven exclaimed, flying closer to the ground. He couldn't believe his luck. There, curled up on the dirt, was the most valuable item he had ever laid eyes on. It was worth hundreds of trinkets and treasures. Maybe even thousands.

I'm just going to borrow this, he thought, stuffing the parchment in his bag. *I'm sure Longtooth won't mind. And if he does, hey, I'll make him a deal.*

Rizzo smiled and quickly flew away. Today was turning out to be a very good day.

Just this morning, he had visited Longtooth the Lion with one of his best deals yet.

"It's a brand-new Speedor wheel. Powerful as can be!" Rizzo had said, presenting Longtooth with a large round stone. It shimmered with blue CHI energy. "Let's make a deal. For you, half off!"

Longtooth wasn't as enthusiastic. "You sneaky thief," he had growled. "That's *my* Speedor wheel. It went missing last month!"

After a heated shouting match, Longtooth had stalked away with the Speedor wheel in hand. He had managed to get it back for just three trinkets and treasures—a very fair deal, if Rizzo said so himself.

That was when the Raven had spotted it.

A curled parchment was lying on the ground near Longtooth's guard post. It looked normal enough. But scrawled across the top in big letters, it read MONTHLY CHI DELIVERY SCHEDULE.

Rizzo realized it was a map of all the CHI delivery routes the Lions were planning to take that month. Anyone who had this scroll could plan ambushes and thefts for weeks! Of course, the Lions could change the schedule, if they noticed the parchment was missing. But if they didn't notice . . . well, a lot of CHI could wind up in the hands of a clever bunch of thieves.

So now, Rizzo was flying back as fast as his wings could carry him to the Ravens' Camp. A devious smile spread across his face. *I could use the map for myself*, he thought. *But I'd need other Ravens to help me ambush the Lions. And then I'd have to split the profits! No,*

I've got a better idea. It's time for a good old-fashioned auction.

Rizzo was not popular, even for a member of his tribe. Where most Ravens had some depths to which they would not sink, Rizzo had none. Other animals said that he was dishonest, a cheat, a thief, someone who would sell his own grandmother if the price was right. He had to admit they were right about the first three. As for Grandma, he always made sure she got a cut whenever he sold her . . . a small cut, but still, it was something. And one thing no one could deny was that he knew how to make a deal.

Rizzo quietly put out the word that the parchment was up for sale, starting with the Crocodiles. Then he let the Wolves know, too. An auction was no good with only one bidder. As he landed in the field chosen for the auction site, he saw Crooler the Crocodile and Windra the Wolf stalking up to the clearing.

"What's *she* doing here?" Windra snarled, looking Crooler up and down.

"I would ask the same thing," Crooler said, her eyes narrowing at Rizzo. "I thought this was a private sale."

"It is," Rizzo insisted. "A private *auction*. Just you two—no one else. Only my best clients."

Rizzo smiled. "Now, who would like to make me the first offer?"

"Where's the parchment?" Windra asked. "Show it to us first."

Rizzo gulped. "Well, I don't have it with me," he said. "How dumb do you think I am?"

Crooler started to answer, but then changed her mind. "Fine. Let's get this over with," she said. "I bid five trinkets and treasures."

"Ten," said Windra.

"Twenty," snapped Crooler.

"I meant ten a month for the rest of your life," Windra hissed.

"I meant twenty a week for the rest of your life," Crooler countered.

Windra leaned in close to Rizzo. "Sell it to me, or there won't *be* a rest of your life."

Rizzo shuddered.

"Stop bidding, *Wolf*," Crooler threatened.

Windra bared her teeth. "Make me."

"This is getting us nowhere," Crooler said angrily. "I don't like your *auction*, Rizzo. There are other ways to settle this." She stalked away.

Windra watched her go, and then slowly turned toward the Raven. "You know, the pack can be a good friend," she smiled at Rizzo. "Suppose you needed a little . . . protection. Worriz and the Wolves would be happy to take care of that for you. All you have to do is give me that parchment."

Rizzo fluttered into the air. He didn't like having a Wolf's jaws quite so close. "Ravens don't give things away," he whined. "It's against the law."

Windra's smile widened. On her face, it was a frightening expression. "And Wolves don't take 'no' for an answer."

Rizzo flew higher, out of reach. "Uh . . . I've gotta go. Things to do. Deals to make. See you later," he said quickly.

Windra watched him fly away. Then she left, too. Neither of them noticed the figure keeping an eye on them silently from the woods. He was covered in mud to mask his scent. Once Crooler and Windra were out of sight, the figure trotted off after Rizzo.

Rizzo landed on a high rock near the mountains. He had never been in the middle of a deal this big, or this dangerous, before. Two of the nastiest females in Chima both wanted this parchment, and they would go *through* him to get it if necessary. Normally, Rizzo stored all his goods-for-sale in a hollow tree near the Ravens' Camp. But this parchment was too hot to keep in any old tree. He carefully tucked the paper into a crack near the bottom of the rock.

Then he decided to check on his other treasures. *Maybe I'll make a few simple deals to clear my head*, he thought. *Nothing like a good bargain to calm my nerves.*

Rizzo flew down into the woods toward the hollow tree where he kept his best stuff. He knew the way by heart and didn't even bother watching where he flew. So he was quite surprised when he smacked headfirst into a tree.

"Holy Razoli!" cried Rizzo, rubbing his head. "Where did that tree come from?"

After the world stopped spinning, Rizzo noticed something. It wasn't just any tree he had collided with. It was *his* hollow tree. But this wasn't where it always was in the forest. Somebody had moved his tree! Frantic, he peered through a knothole. All his stuff was gone!

"Don't you hate it when trees move?"

Rizzo felt a chill run through him. He turned to see Crooler leaning casually against a rock.

"Good thing your junk wasn't stolen," she said. "It's just scattered around the woods. Sometimes my boys get a little . . . messy."

"Aw, come on," Rizzo groaned. "The other Ravens will have found all my good stuff by now."

"Well, accidents do happen," Crooler said, walking closer. "It would be a shame if any more *accidents* happened, right?"

"Yeah . . ." Rizzo gulped.

"But a parchment can buy protection. So more accidents don't happen. Get it?" she said.

"G-G-Got it," Rizzo stammered.

"Good," said Crooler. "You know what to do."

Rizzo flew home. Now he was *really* worried. If he gave the parchment to Windra, Crooler would drop a

tree on him. But if he gave it to Crooler, he would have the Wolf Pack chasing him forever. And if he *gave* it to anyone, instead of selling it, Razar and the Ravens would laugh him out of the nest!

By that evening, Rizzo still hadn't figured out what to do. He decided to sleep on it. Maybe he would come up with the best deal ever for the parchment after a full night's sleep.

All night, Rizzo had bad dreams. He kept thinking Windra and Crooler had come to the Raven Camp. They were searching for the parchment. When they couldn't

find it, he dreamed that they decided to take *him* instead. Then they got into an argument over who got to "persuade" him to talk first.

When Rizzo woke up the next morning, the camp was in chaos. There were Wolf footprints all over the ground below the nests. Someone had dripped swamp water on Razar's ledgers. And the Ravens were flying about in a panic. Shocked, Rizzo realized it hadn't been a dream: The Wolves and the Crocodiles had actually shown up. They had ransacked the Raven Camp looking for the parchment!

That's it, Rizzo thought. *This parchment is too hot for even a Raven to hold on to. I've got to get rid of it!*

Suddenly, Rizzo realized the answer to all his problems. He just had to do what Ravens did best: swindle! It was so simple, he wondered why he hadn't thought of it before.

"I'll sell them both fake copies of the CHI delivery schedule!" he exclaimed.

Rizzo set to work forging new schedules on pieces of parchment. He made two: one for the Crocodiles, and one for the Wolves. They were completely different from each other, so the two sides wouldn't wind up both at the same site waiting to ambush the Lions. Of course,

neither of the forgeries used information from the real schedule. That way, it wasn't like he was giving anything of real value to either side. The Crocodiles would be happy. The Wolves would be happy. And the Ravens wouldn't kick Rizzo out of the nest for breaking the cardinal rule to never *give* anything away. That made Rizzo happy.

When he was done, Rizzo took one copy to the Wolf Pack. He made a quick deal with Windra: the parchment in exchange for the Wolves' "continued protection."

Then he took the other copy to the swamp and gave it to Crooler in exchange for more "protection."

On his way back to camp, Rizzo felt like a winner. After all, what could go wrong? Even if all the ambushes were failures, both tribes would just assume the Lions had discovered a copy of the schedule had been stolen and so changed their plans. None of it could be traced back to Rizzo.

Phew, Rizzo thought. *That's the last auction I'm holding for a while.*

Three days later, Wilhurt the Wolf was very angry. He had just spent four hours hiding in the woods with the rest of the pack, waiting to ambush the Lions' CHI delivery. But the Lions never showed up. Frustrated, Wilhurt ordered the pack back to camp when they bumped into Crawley and the Crocodiles.

"Lost?" he asked Crawley with a sneer.

"No," Crawley snapped. "We were waiting to ambush Laval and take some CHI, but he must have made a new

plan. Either that, or the schedule we got from Rizzo is wrong."

"The schedule *you* got . . . ?" Wilhurt exclaimed. "What are you talking about? *We* got the CHI schedule from Rizzo. It said to wait by the twin oak trees today, but we never saw any Lions."

"Ours said to wait by the bend in the creek," Crawley said. His eyes narrowed. "Are you thinking what I'm thinking?"

"I smell a Raven," Wilhurt snarled.

The next day, Rizzo was just about to head to the Beavers' dam to sell them some wood when he heard rustling in the bushes behind him. Rizzo tried to take off, but before he could get away, a hand grabbed his leg. Then a second hand grabbed his other leg.

It was Windra and Crooler. And they didn't look happy.

"Uh, hello," Rizzo said. "What can I do for you charming ladies today?"

Windra growled. "Those CHI schedules you sold us—"

"Were fakes!" Crooler finished.

"What?" exclaimed Rizzo, putting on his most innocent expression. "I'm shocked. Shocked! I promise you, I won't rest until I find out what happened."

"I promise you won't rest, either," Windra said through gritted teeth.

"Take us to the real parchment now, Raven," said Crooler, "or else."

"Or else?" gulped Rizzo.

"You're a fast talker," Crooler said. "Try talking when your beak's upside down."

No matter how much Rizzo hated giving things away, he *really* didn't want to find out what Windra and Crooler were capable of. He led them to the rock where he had hidden the parchment. Windra flipped it over and grabbed the paper. Crooler snatched it out of her hand.

"Give me that!" snapped Windra.

"Make me," taunted Crooler.

"Fine," Windra said. "Then let's look at it together. We're your *allies*, remember? We'll help you attack the Lions. That is, if we're still on the same side."

Begrudgingly, Crooler allowed Windra to look over her shoulder as she read the parchment. *"Monthly Schedule,"* she read aloud. *"Task One: Clean out caves. Task Two: Train with Leonidas. Task Three: Trick Wolves, Crocodiles, and Rizzo with a fake parchment . . ."*

Crooler crumpled the paper up in her claws. "This isn't a CHI delivery schedule—it's a to-do list!" she cried.

"But I don't understand," Rizzo sputtered, snatching away the parchment. "It was real. I saw it with my own two eyes. And I left it right here!"

As the three animals argued, none of them noticed the small group of Lions hidden off to the side, laughing quietly.

"See?" Longtooth said to his soldiers. "I told you I would handle it."

"But how did you know where the parchment was hidden?" one of the Lions asked.

"It was easy," Longtooth explained. "I knew that sneaky Raven was behind it. But as slippery as Ravens are, they're no match for a Lion's hunting skills. I just waited until Rizzo went to sell it, which I knew he

would, and followed him to where he had hidden it. I switched out the real parchment yesterday. It was a piece of cake."

"Looks like you taught that Raven a lesson." The Lions grinned as they heard Rizzo trying to sweet-talk Crooler and Windra into believing it was all a big misunderstanding.

"Now, ladies," Rizzo was saying, "don't worry. I'm sure we can work something out."

"You're right, we will," Crooler said as she and Windra walked closer.

With a squawk, Rizzo raced away as fast as his legs would carry him. Windra and Crooler chased close behind.

"You won't get away with this, Raven!" they both shouted after him.

One of the Lions looked at Longtooth. "Think he'll be all right?" he asked.

Longtooth nodded. "Eh, he'll be fine," he said. "After all, if there's one thing we know Rizzo is an expert at, it's making a deal."